Hotwife: Streamer Girlfriend
Ms Naughtee

HOTWIFE: STREAMER GIRLFRIEND

First edition. May 16, 2024.

ISBN: 979-8230791614

Written by Ms Naughtee.

Also by Ms Naughtee

A History In Love
A History In Love

BLACKED
Blacked Friday: A Cuck/Hotwife Novel
Black Friday 2: Blacker and Darker

Hotwife
Cucked 2 Book Collection: Backyard Pool Party & A Blast From The
Past
Hotwife: Sexy Beach Vacation
Hotwife: Streamer Girlfriend
Cuck: Backyard Pool Party
Hotwife: Taking It All
Hotwife: Firefighter Fantasy
Hotwife: Halloween Hijinks!
Hotwife: Hypnosis Fantasy
Hotwife: Boudoir Photo Shoot
Hotwife: A Very Merry XXXmas
Hotwife: The New Year's Eve Party

Hotwife: Shared At Home
Cucked: A Blast From The Past
Hotwife: The St. Patrick's Party
Cheating: My Unfaithful Wife
Cheating: My Wife And Best Friend
Cheating: The Age Gap Affair
Cheating: My Husband Doesn't Know
Cheating: Behind Closed Blinds
Hotwife: The Tattoo Artist
Hotwife: At The Cottage
Hotwife: Cool Hiking
Cheating: The Boudoir Photographer
Hotwife: Hypnosis Hedonism
Cheating: My Neighbor's Son
Hotwife: Shared at Sea
Hotwife: Sexy Beach Resort
Hotwife: The Nude Beach
Hotwife: The Shower Scene
Cheating: Dark Desires
Cheating: Cold Revenge

Lesbian
The Christmas Party: A Lesbian Romance Novel
Lesbian: My Forever Valentine
Girls Trip: A Lesbian Fantasy
Lesbian Pool Party

Love Letters
Love Letters: A Young Love Story
Love Letters 2: The Second Chapter

Love Letters 3: A New Beginning

MILF
MILF: Crossing The Age Gap
MILF: On The Naughty List
MILF: The Babysitter's Secret
MILF: My Busty Neighbour
MILF: No One Can Know
Cougar: Single & Ready to Mingle
The Cougar and Her Cub: An Age Gap Fantasy
MILF: Eyes on the Prize
MILF: Full-Body Inspection
The MILF & The Pool Boy
MILF: The Cougar & Her Prey
MILF: An Unexpected Hookup
MILF: Public Seduction
MILF: A Wild Ride

Pregnancy
Pregnant: Suspense and Secrets
Pregnant: The Best Christmas Present

Threesome
The Threesome: MMF
Gangbang: By The Christmas Tree
Gangbang: A First Time For Everything
Sexy St. Patrick's Day: 2 Book Collection
Gangbang: St. Patrick's Day

Gangbang After Dark: An Interracial Smut Novella
Silent Springs Secrets
Gangbang: Til Dawn Do Us Part
Gangbang: At The Art Studio
Gangbang: At The Nude Beach

Trans
Trans Romance: A Dark First Time (M To F)
Trans Romance: A Friendship Gone Right (Or Wrong)
Trans Romance: My Old Crush

Standalone
The Genie of Love

Table of Contents

Hello to all my readers, new and old!

I wanted to say thank you so much for reading this book. It is a labour of love for me to work on my craft!

As a show of gratitude for you all enabling me to live my dream, please visit my Substack page. I often give out free e-books for my fans over there. And the best part is, there is ZERO cost. It will always be 100% free to follow me and my stories over there.

If you'd like to claim your free e-book, head to
https://msnaughtee.substack.com/

-Ms Naughtee <3

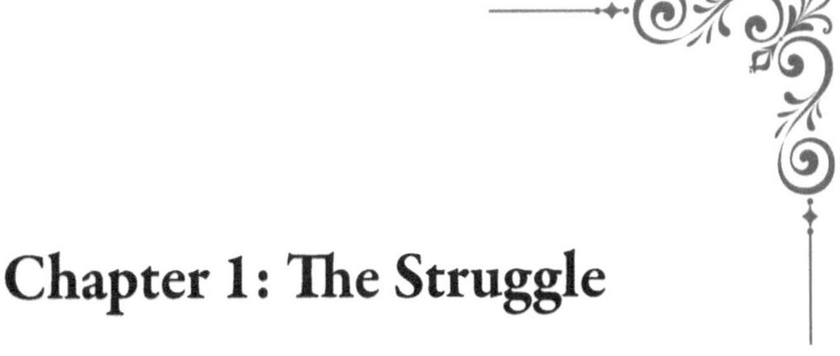

Chapter 1: The Struggle

Sunlight streamed through the expansive windows of the living room, painting the plush rug with golden stripes. I stretched luxuriously in the king-sized bed, the only sound the gentle chirping of birds outside. In the distance, the hum of the coffee maker promised a much-needed morning jolt.

A sigh drifted down the hallway, pulling me fully awake. Valerie sat hunched over her computer in the makeshift streaming room, her usual vibrant spirit dimmed. Her hair, typically a shocking burst of pink, now lay limp around her shoulders, mirroring the slump of her posture.

"Rough night, babe?" I asked, padding down the hallway and leaning against the doorway frame.

Valerie glanced up, the exhaustion in her emerald eyes a stark contrast to the cheerful floral wallpaper of the room. "Almost done with tonight's stream," she muttered, her voice hoarse. She'd been up all night for this one. "Just gotta thank the few viewers who hung out."

I peeked at the screen. The chat window scrolled by with a disheartening slowness, a couple of usernames punctuated by the occasional lonely "hi." The donation counter remained stubbornly empty.

Though a single income household, my established career allowed for a more comfortable living situation than the cramped apartment we initially considered. It felt extravagant, but I wanted to support her dream.

"How many viewers tonight?" I asked, stepping into the room and placing a reassuring hand on her shoulder.

"Maybe a dozen," she mumbled, leaning into my touch. "Mostly lurkers who haven't even spoken."

The truth hit me like a physical blow. We'd prepared for initial struggles, but reality was harsh. My savings account, once comfortably plump, was slowly shrinking, replaced by a nagging unease.

"Hey," I said, forcing a smile. "Building an audience takes time. You're funny and talented, you just gotta stay positive."

Valerie offered a weak smile in return. "I know, I know. But bills don't get paid in ramen, and the credit card for this fancy streaming equipment is starting to sweat."

Guilt gnawed at me. The financial burden shouldn't be hers to bear. Maybe I should've steered her towards a more practical path. But seeing the sheer joy and passion gaming brought Valerie, I couldn't bring myself to do it.

"We'll figure it out," I promised, pulling her into a hug. "Maybe we can talk to my accountant about tax optimization strategies for streamers..."

Valerie chuckled, a flicker of life returning to her eyes. "Absolutely not, Mr. Moneybags. This is my dream, and I'm not giving up that easily. You can't always be figuring out everything for me."

I kissed the top of her head, the determination in her voice a spark of hope. We were in this together, the struggles and the triumphs, both unsure of what the future held, but determined to face it as a team. Twitch stardom might be a distant peak, but as long as Valerie had her fire, I'd be her sherpa, carrying the financial weight so she could focus on the climb.

The exhaustion finally caught up to Valerie. After hitting "End Stream," she let out a long sigh that echoed in the small room. The vibrant pink of her hair, usually a symbol of her effervescent personality, seemed muted under the harsh fluorescent lights.

I watched her for a moment, the weight of unspoken worry heavy in the air. She deserved better than this constant struggle. The silence stretched between us until she spoke, her voice barely a whisper.

"I think I'm going to crash for a nap," she mumbled, pushing back from the desk. "Amy texted, she's brewing some fancy coffee later today and wants to catch up. I told her I'd go hang out with her for a bit."

I nodded, forcing a smile. "Sounds good, baby. Go have your nap first, you look exhausted."

She agreed that she was, offering a small, tired smile in return before disappearing down the hallway. She struggled, slow in her walk, maintaining her balance by keeping her hand against the wall as she glided down the hallway, molasses-like.

I hung out and read some news, before making myself breakfast and relaxing with my first cup of coffee. It was a great start to my day, other than worrying about Val. I didn't mind relaxing by myself, either with Netflix or a good book.

Later that day, Valerie got up and quickly got ready. She let me know she was already leaving, quickly calling out to me, "I'm heading out!"

"Okay babe, enjoy it! See you later!" I yelled back in response.

The silence that followed was deafening. I wandered into the kitchen, pouring myself a cup of the now lukewarm coffee. The silence seemed to amplify the doubts that had been gnawing at me.

Was this really the right path for her? Was I being selfish, letting her chase a dream that so far seemed more like a pipe dream? The question hung heavy in the air, unanswered.

Hours bled into one another. The house felt empty without Valerie's usual bursts of laughter and enthusiastic chatter. I tried to focus on work emails, but the words blurred on the screen. Thoughts of Valerie's dwindling savings and mounting debt swirled in my head.

The sound of the front door opening jolted me out of my reverie. Valerie walked in, a hint of colour back in her cheeks. She carried a small paper bag, the aroma of freshly baked cookies wafting in behind her.

"Hey, you," she said, her voice brighter than it had been all day. "Amy whipped up these cookies. Stress relief for both of us, apparently."

I managed a smile, taking the bag from her hands. "Sounds like a good plan."

Despite the effort, my heart felt heavy. The few hours alone had only served to solidify the worry in my gut. We needed a solution, and I wasn't sure what it was. Looking at Valerie's hopeful face, however, I knew one thing for certain. We'd face it together, whatever the future held.

"So," I started, pulling her close, "tell me all about Amy's fancy coffee and whatever crazy gossip she spilled."

Valerie launched into a story about a hilarious mishap at Amy's work, her voice gradually regaining its usual enthusiasm. For now, I pushed my worries aside, focusing on the sound of her laughter, a small beacon of hope in the uncertain landscape ahead. All the worries she'd had earlier in the day seemed to have disappeared completely.

Chapter 2: The Proposal

The next day, she told me she had a plan.

"I think I know what to do to solve all our problems," Valerie declared the next day, a determined glint in her emerald eyes. The pink strands of her hair seemed to bounce with newfound energy, a stark contrast to the defeated slump of the previous evening.

"What is it, babe?" I asked, leaning forward in anticipation. Curiosity battled with a sliver of apprehension. Could she really have formulated a solution so quickly? Part of me doubted it, but the hope in her eyes kept me from dismissing it entirely.

Valerie cleared her throat, taking a deep breath. "You know how I went to Amy's yesterday? Well, they were talking about something interesting..." she trailed off, a hesitant blush creeping up her cheeks.

"Interesting?" I prompted, a flicker of unease flickering across my chest. "What kind of interesting?"

"Okay, so you know how some streamers use this platform called OnlyFans?" she blurted, her voice rushing slightly.

My stomach lurched. OnlyFans. The name had swirled around the internet in recent years, a platform notorious for its adult content. The image it conjured clashed violently with the bubbly, enthusiastic gamer girl I knew.

"Hold on a sec," I interrupted, my voice tighter than intended. "OnlyFans? Are you seriously considering...?"

Valerie held up a hand, silencing me before I could finish the thought. "Look, I know what you're thinking," she said, her voice surprisingly firm despite the blush blooming across her face. "But it's not just about...well, you know."

"Not just about what?" I pressed, trying to keep my tone neutral.

"There are a lot of creators out there who use it to offer exclusive content," she explained, her voice gaining confidence. "Behind-the-scenes glimpses, early access to streams, Q&A sessions... things like that. It's a way to build a closer connection with their fan base and reward their most dedicated followers."

A spark of logic flickered through the initial shock. Valerie had a point. It could be a way to offer her dedicated viewers something extra, a way to monetize the loyal following she was already working towards building.

"So, you're thinking of using it to, what, offer exclusive gaming sessions or blooper reels?" I asked, cautiously testing the waters of this idea. I was still worried about where this was going.

Valerie's face lit up. "Exactly! Plus, it's a way to directly generate income from the fans who already support me. Imagine, if even a fraction of my current viewers subscribed on OnlyFans, it could make a huge difference."

The truth of her words settled in my gut. It was a gamble, yes, and the idea of her participating on a platform with such a reputation made me uneasy. But the alternative – watching her dream slowly die, the weight of financial burden crushing her spirit – was far worse.

"There's just one more thing," Valerie added, her voice dropping to a whisper. She leaned in closer, a mischievous glint in her emerald eyes. "Let's be honest, babe, I wouldn't be completely opposed to using a little... sex appeal to our advantage either."

A wave of heat flooded my cheeks. This wasn't just about exclusive content anymore. There was a whole other layer to this proposition, one that sent a jolt of conflicting emotions through me. Was I comfortable with Valerie exploring this side of herself online? Could our relationship handle the potential changes it might bring?

Despite the uncertainty, one thing was clear. Valerie's passion for streaming was reignited, and this unconventional path was a fire she was determined to stoke. Whether I liked it or not, it seemed like we were both about to embark on a whole new adventure.

"Valerie," I started, my voice tight, "I don't know if I'm comfortable with that. This platform... it's not exactly known for wholesome content."

"I know, I know," she said, her voice softening. "But listen, it wouldn't be anything X-rated. Maybe some tasteful cosplay, flirty gamer banter, subscriber-only access to some of my workout routines..." Her voice trailed off, searching my face for a reaction.

The image of Valerie in cosplay, a playful wink at the camera, was less horrifying than I initially imagined. But the thought of her workout routines being available to a paying audience still left me unsettled. It felt... intrusive, a line I wasn't sure I wanted crossed.

"Look," Valerie continued, her hand reaching for mine, "I wouldn't do anything I wasn't comfortable with. And besides, wouldn't it be a turn-on knowing you're the only one who gets to see the real me, the one without the internet persona?"

A flicker of heat rose in my cheeks. The truth was, the thought of her flirting with an audience, even in a playful way, did stir a possessive streak within me. But her last point hit a nerve. Maybe, just maybe, there could be a way to navigate this together, to set boundaries that protected her comfort and mine. She was right. Something about this was hot.

"Maybe," I conceded hesitantly, "but we need to talk about ground rules. What kind of content are you comfortable with? How much... exposure are you okay with?"

Valerie's smile widened, relief flooding her features. "That's exactly what I wanted to hear!" She pulled out her laptop, a flurry of excitement replacing her earlier nervousness. "Let's brainstorm some ideas together. We can figure out a way to make this work for both of us, something that fuels the stream and keeps your jealous side at bay."

The last part came with a playful wink, and despite the lingering unease, a small part of me couldn't help but smile back. We were in uncharted territory for sure, but one thing was clear: Valerie wouldn't be venturing into this alone. We'd navigate this new reality, this unconventional path to her streaming dream, together, one awkward conversation and carefully crafted boundary at a time. Valerie pulled out her laptop and began taking notes.

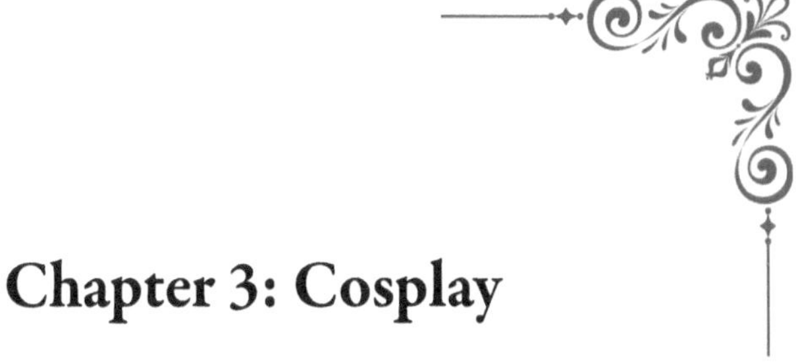

Chapter 3: Cosplay

The air crackled with nervous anticipation as Valerie disappeared into the bedroom. The hum of the webcam filled the silence, a constant reminder of the audience waiting on the other side. I fidgeted with the remote, the usual pre-stream jitters amplified by the events of the past week.

Valerie's foray into the world of camming had been a gamble, one that paid off beyond our wildest expectations. Her infectious enthusiasm and undeniable charisma, coupled with the playful flirtation that came naturally to her, had turned her stream into a sizzling success. Viewership numbers skyrocketed, donations poured in, and whispers of her growing popularity echoed across online forums.

But the real surprise was the explosion of interest in her newly launched OnlyFans page. The carefully curated photos – a tasteful blend of cosplay and playful pin-up style – had captivated a dedicated audience. The financial burden that had been weighing us down started to feel lighter with each new subscriber.

Tonight's theme was "Legendary Warriors," and Valerie had promised a triple threat. The anticipation in the chat was palpable, a mix of playful speculation and suggestive emojis. Then, the bedroom door swung open, and the air hung heavy with a collective gasp from the unseen audience.

Standing there, bathed in the soft glow of fairy lights, was a vision of fiery power. The unmistakable red hair, styled in elaborate braids, framed a face painted with fierce war paint. The skimpy leather armor, more suggestion than coverage, clung to her curves, leaving little to the imagination. Valerie, channeling a certain fiery princess from a popular fantasy game, looked like she'd stepped straight out of the screen.

The chat exploded in a frenzy. "Damn, Valerie!" "Holy smokes!" "That cosplay is killer!" The donation counter ticked up at an alarming rate. Even I, a seasoned observer of her beauty, felt a jolt of desire course through me. She radiated an intoxicating blend of confidence and playful sensuality that was impossible to resist.

Over the next hour, Valerie transformed. A sleek, cybernetic bodysuit materialised, the blue glow of strategically placed lights highlighting the sleek lines of her body. Then, with a flourish, she donned the flowing white robes and flowing silver hair of a powerful healer, her eyes twinkling with mischief.

Each costume change brought a fresh wave of excitement and a surge in subscriptions on her OnlyFans page. By the end of the stream, her cheeks were flushed with exertion and a satisfied smile played on her lips. She'd not only entertained her audience, she'd taken a significant leap towards financial security and, in the process, discovered a potent new side to her online persona.

Later that night, as we lay tangled in the sheets, the afterglow of the stream lingering in the air, I looked at Valerie with a newfound appreciation. The girl who once nervously navigated the world of gaming had blossomed into a confident, captivating woman. The fear and uncertainty of the past had melted away, replaced by a spark of ambition and a healthy dose of self-assuredness.

"You did amazing tonight," I murmured, tracing a finger down the curve of her back.

Valerie grinned, a playful glint in her emerald eyes. "Thanks, babe. Though, I have to admit, it was a little nerve-wracking showing off that much skin."

I chuckled. "Nervously confident, huh? Seems like a winning combination for your viewers." My voice dipped lower. "And for me, too."

A blush crept up her cheeks, but her eyes held a challenge. "Just wait," she whispered, leaning in closer. "I have a few more tricks up my sleeve for next week's stream."

The promise hung heavy in the air, a delicious tease of what was to come. The world of camming might have been uncharted territory, but one thing was certain: with Valerie leading the way, it was going to be a thrilling, and undeniably steamy, adventure.

We spent the entire night exchanging the deepest, hottest kisses I've ever experienced. We couldn't keep away from each other. I climbed on top, in the silence of the night, and we made gentle, sweet love for what felt like hours.

Chapter 4: Trying More

The glow of the computer screen cast an ethereal light on Valerie's face as she scrolled through the endless stream of comments. A mix of excitement and apprehension bubbled in my gut. The past few weeks had been a whirlwind. Her stream viewership had hit new highs, her OnlyFans boasted a dedicated fan base, and the financial pressure had finally started to ease.

However, a subtle shift in the online chatter had begun to niggle at me. The playful compliments about her cosplay were becoming more explicit, the veiled requests for "more" growing bolder. A video call notification popped up, revealing Amy's grinning face.

"Hey lovebirds," she chirped, her voice laced with excitement. "Did you see the latest comments from your top donors on OnlyFans? Those guys are practically begging for a show!"

Valerie bit her lip, a mischievous glint in her emerald eyes. "Yeah, I saw. They're getting a little... specific."

"Specific is good, Val!" Amy declared, leaning closer to the camera. "Those are your paying customers, and they know what they want. You're giving them a taste of the forbidden fruit, now it's time to peel back the rest."

My stomach clenched. Amy's bluntness was both refreshing and unsettling in this situation. There was no denying the financial appeal of catering to these requests, but a part of me rebelled at the thought of Valerie stripping down further, exposing more of herself to a faceless audience.

"I don't know, Amy," I interjected hesitantly. "It feels like things are moving a little fast. What if she's not comfortable with..."

"Relax, Mr. Grumpy," Valerie cut me off with a playful shove. "I can handle myself. Besides, the fans made me, and keeping them happy is part of the game, right?"

"Happy, yes," I conceded, choosing my words carefully. "But not at the expense of your comfort or safety. Remember, we set boundaries for a reason."

Valerie sighed, a flicker of doubt clouding her usually bright eyes. "I know, babe. It's just... the money is tempting. And frankly, a part of me is curious to see how far I can push this whole persona."

My heart sank. The curiosity she mentioned was an unfamiliar glint in her eyes, a thrill seeker's spark that worried me. I wanted to be supportive, but the line between confidence and exploitation felt dangerously thin.

"Look," I suggested, hoping to find a compromise. "Why don't we set some ground rules for this 'more'? Maybe some tasteful lingerie shots, a tease here and there, nothing too explicit?"

Valerie and Amy exchanged glances, a silent conversation passing between them. Finally, Amy spoke, her voice softer now. "That's actually a good idea, (your name). You two can set some boundaries, something you're both okay with. Remember, Val, you're in control."

Valerie nodded, a thoughtful expression on her face. "Yeah, maybe we can find a middle ground. Something that keeps the fans happy but doesn't make me feel uncomfortable."

The conversation continued, exploring different possibilities. A sense of relief washed over me as Valerie outlined some ideas, sticking to the boundaries we'd previously discussed. But even with these precautions in place, a nagging worry remained. The path she was walking was a double-edged sword. Success and empowerment resided on one side, risk and potential exploitation on the other. All I could do was be there for her, help her through this confusing time in our lives together, and hope that the thrill of online fame wouldn't consume the essence of the girl I knew and loved.

As the conversation with Amy ended, a new thought bloomed in Valerie's eyes. "Hey, what about..." she began, a hint of experimentation in her voice.

"About what, babe?" I asked, curious about the sudden shift in her focus.

"There's talk about artistic nudes on OnlyFans," she explained, scrolling through a few reference photos on her phone. "Not explicit, just tasteful, artistic shots that play with light and shadow. Like a body study, you know?"

Intrigue battled with apprehension in my gut. The idea was... different. Not necessarily bad, but a whole new layer to consider. "Artistic nudes, huh?"

"Yeah!" Valerie enthused, showing me some examples. "They're beautiful, really. And some creators use them to offer exclusive content to their top subscribers."

A flicker of a different kind of heat sparked within me. The thought of Valerie's form captured in a tasteful, artistic way was surprisingly arousing. Maybe this artistic route could be a way for her to explore this new persona without sacrificing her comfort.

"That's... actually an interesting idea," I admitted, surprised by my own openness. "As long as you're comfortable with it, of course."

"Me?" Valerie laughed, a playful glint in her eyes. "Trust me, if anyone can pull off artistic nudes, it's me. I mean, have you seen the lighting in our bedroom?" She winked, a playful challenge in her tone.

The tension from the previous conversation seemed to dissipate, replaced by a sense of shared exploration. Maybe, just maybe, this artistic venture could be a creative outlet for both of us. There was a fine line to walk, for sure, but with open communication and clear boundaries, perhaps we could navigate it together.

"Alright, then," I conceded, a smile tugging at my lips. "Let's brainstorm some artistic lighting set-ups. Just promise me one thing – safety first. No crazy contortions or risky positions, okay?"

Valerie rolled her eyes playfully. "Relax, Mr. Safety Patrol. I wouldn't do anything to hurt myself. Now, about that lighting..."

And so, the conversation shifted once more, this time filled with playful ideas and creative inspiration. The anxiety that had previously gripped me melted away, replaced by a sense of cautious optimism. I wasn't sure what the future held. And I still wasn't completely comfortable with this. That said, maybe this artistic endeavour could be a thrilling and empowering experience, both for Valerie and for us as a couple.

Chapter 5: Success

Everything was going well. Almost too well, in fact. Valerie's ideas for tasteful nudes sent her from bringing in a nice little side income to the equivalent of a full-time job. She'd probably be making even more money had she gotten on this trend earlier, but she was doing quite well, regardless.

Valerie slammed her laptop shut, a triumphant grin splitting her face. "Did you see those new subscriber numbers? We're killing it!" She tossed her head back, the golden light streaming through the window catching the glint of expensive new jewelry adorning her wrist.

I shifted uncomfortably on the couch, the cheerful chirp of her notification ringtone starting to grate on my nerves. "It's great, Val, really. But maybe we should slow down a bit?"

Valerie's smile faltered for a second, replaced by a flicker of annoyance. "Slow down? Why? We've finally hit our stride. This is the kind of money I've always dreamed of making."

"Yeah, but..." I hesitated, searching for the right words. "Those messages you got for the 'exclusive' stuff, they're getting pretty intense, wouldn't you say?"

A dismissive snort escaped Valerie's lips. "People pay a premium for a reason. We're just giving the customers what they want. Besides," she leaned in, her voice conspiratorial, "have you seen the kind of money those top creators are pulling in? It's insane. We could be living like royalty in a year, first class flights, designer everything..."

I winced internally. The fire in Valerie's eyes wasn't just ambition anymore, it was greed, a hunger that worried me deeply. "Don't you think there's something...vulnerable about locking away the best stuff? Like we're cheapening ourselves?"

Valerie scoffed. "Vulnerable? Honey, this is business. We're building an empire, one spicy photo at a time. Think about it, wouldn't it be amazing to never have to worry about anything again? We could travel the world, you could finally quit that soul-crushing job you hate..."

The way she used my own frustrations against me stung. I knew she had a point, but the path she was on felt reckless, a dangerous gamble with something far more precious than money. "But what if it's not enough, Val? What if the line between exclusive and...well, something else, keeps blurring?"

Valerie waved my concerns away dismissively. "We'll cross that bridge when we come to it. Right now, we're in the driver's seat. This is liberation, babe, not some kind of prison. We're calling the shots, for once."

The air crackled with unspoken tension. I loved Valerie, but the woman staring back at me with dollar signs in her eyes felt like a stranger. A cold dread settled in my stomach. This wasn't the future I'd envisioned together, and the growing distance between us felt like a chasm waiting to swallow me whole.

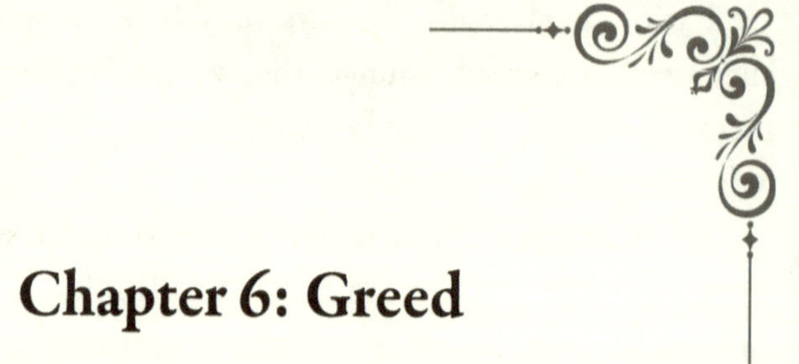

Chapter 6: Greed

The champagne flute trembled in Valerie's hand, the clinking of glasses a discordant note in the tense silence. The celebratory dinner for a million subscribers felt like a funeral feast. My worried glances bounced off Valerie's mirrored sunglasses, a shield against the emotions I knew simmered beneath.

"A million, can you believe it?" Valerie finally said, her voice laced with an undercurrent of something else – a hunger I couldn't quite place. "We're practically internet royalty now."

I forced a smile, the taste of caviar suddenly metallic on my tongue. "Yeah, it's incredible. We should be proud."

"Should be?" Valerie's voice sharpened, a glint of something dangerous flickering behind the mirrored lenses. "We *are* proud. But shouldn't we be aiming higher? Look at the competition, raking in millions with..." she trailed off, a pointed look in my direction.

I knew exactly what she was implying. The "exclusive content" requests had become a constant drumbeat, the pressure to push boundaries a suffocating fog. A cold dread settled in my gut.

"Val, we've come so far with tasteful content," I said, my voice firm despite the tremor in my hands. "Don't you think that's enough?"

Valerie scoffed, a humourless laugh that echoed off the cavernous restaurant walls. "Enough? Honey, a million might sound like a lot, but in this game, it's just the starting line. Imagine a private jet, a beachfront villa...all within reach if we just..." she trailed off again, her voice dropping to a seductive purr, "give the people what they really want."

"And what exactly do they want?" I countered, my voice rising with a mix of anger and fear. "Because right now, it feels like you're the one who's hungry, not them."

Valerie's eyes narrowed, the glint behind her sunglasses turning into a steely glare. "Don't be naive. This is a business, and business is booming. We'd be fools not to capitalize on it."

"But at what cost, Val?" I pressed, leaning forward, my voice low but urgent. "This isn't just about money anymore. This is about you changing, becoming someone I don't recognize."

A tense silence stretched between us, broken only by the clinking of ice cubes in Valerie's abandoned champagne flute. The air crackled with such a surreal tension.

"Look," Valerie finally said, her voice clipped, "I appreciate your concern, but this is my decision. I'm taking control of my career, my life."

"And what about our life?" I shot back, my voice tinged with desperation. "This wasn't the future we talked about, the future we were building together."

Valerie's jaw clenched, her eyes locked on mine for a long, hard moment. The woman I loved, the woman I'd shared my dreams with, seemed to fade away, replaced by a stranger driven by blind ambition.

"Then maybe," Valerie said, her voice cold and measured, "it's time to re-evaluate what that future looks like."

The weight of her words slammed into me. It was a challenge, a line drawn in the sand. Could I adapt to this new Valerie, or was this the painful end of our shared dream? I stared at her, the woman I loved disappearing behind a glittering veil of ambition, and the answer, heavy and unwelcome, settled in my heart.

I watched, a silent observer to the metamorphosis of the woman I'd loved. This wasn't the future I'd envisioned, and the chilling realization settled in – I might either have to adapt to this new Valerie, or walk away from the life we'd built together.

Valerie's eyes softened a hint, maybe sensing the turmoil building inside me. She sighed, the harsh edge to her voice replaced by a flicker of vulnerability. "Look," she said, "I know this isn't exactly the path we planned. But this kind of money...it could change everything. We wouldn't have to worry about a *thing* anymore."

Her hand reached across the table, hovering over mine. A playful glint flickered back into her eyes. "And hey," she said, "it wouldn't be all bad, right? We could do it together. Think of it as an adventure."

Adventure. A bitter laugh almost escaped me. The image of myself, somehow entangled in her online persona, sent a shiver down my spine.

"Val," I said, my voice gentle but firm, "I appreciate the offer, but you know I can't do that. It would be a disaster – for my career, for our financial security..."

"Security?" Valerie scoffed. "Honey, this is security on steroids! We wouldn't have to worry about that dead-end job of yours anymore. You could finally focus on your art, your passion. Think about it!"

But I was already shaking my head, the weight of responsibility pressing down on me. I was the one with the steady paycheck, the one who'd always grounded our dreams with practicality.

"This isn't just about money," I said, meeting her gaze. "It's about boundaries, about who we are. I can't support this path, not if it means sacrificing what we believe in and the future we planned together."

A heavy silence stretched between us, broken only by the soft murmur of the restaurant. Valerie's hand retreated, the playful glint replaced by a flicker of hurt.

"So," she finally whispered, "what does that mean for us?"

The question hung heavy in the air, a brutal crossroads. I loved Valerie, but the future she envisioned felt like a gilded cage, suffocating everything we held dear. I took a deep breath, the answer a bitter truth to swallow.

"I don't know," I admitted, my voice thick with emotion. "Maybe...maybe we need some time to figure this out."

The celebratory dinner had soured, leaving behind a bitter taste of uncertainty. The million-subscriber milestone, once a victory, now felt like a bridge burning behind us. Our future, once bright with shared dreams, now hung precariously in the balance.

The silence stretched, thick and suffocating. Valerie's hand remained withdrawn, the playful glint in her eyes replaced by a steely resolve that sent shivers down my spine.

"There's another option," she finally said, her voice clipped and devoid of the earlier vulnerability. "Amy mentioned a guy, Kevin, who does this kind of work. She used to work with him; said he's discreet and professional."

A knot of dread formed in my stomach. Amy. My friend, the one who'd initially encouraged Valerie to start the channel, the one who now seemed to be pushing her further down this path.

"Valerie, no," I said, my voice firm despite the tremor running through me. "We don't need to do this. We can figure something else out, something that doesn't involve..." I trailed off, unable to voice the disgust churning in my gut.

"Figure what out?" Valerie countered, her voice laced with a sharp edge. "We have bills to pay, dreams to chase. This is an opportunity, a chance to finally break free from the monotony!"

"But at what cost?" I pleaded, desperation creeping into my voice. "This isn't who we are, Val. Remember all those nights we talked about building something together, something with integrity? This feels like a betrayal of everything we believed in!"

Valerie's gaze hardened. "The world has changed," she said, her voice cold. "Maybe our dreams need to change, too. Look, I appreciate your concerns, but I'm going to do this, with or without you." She paused, a flicker of something akin to pain crossing her features. "If you can't be a part of it, then..." she left the sentence hanging, a heavy silence settling in its wake.

The air crackled with unspoken threats. I knew Valerie. She was stubborn, and when she set her mind on something, it was hard to sway her. The thought of her alone with this "Kevin," navigating this seedy underbelly of the internet, sent a jolt of fear through me.

"You wouldn't," I said, my voice barely a whisper.

Valerie's jaw clenched, but a flicker of defiance remained in her eyes. "Don't underestimate me," she said, her voice a low growl. "I don't need your permission."

The celebratory dinner was a distant memory now, replaced by a bitter reality. I sat across from the woman I loved, but a stranger seemed to stare back, driven by a hunger I couldn't recognize. The future we'd envisioned together lay shattered on the polished restaurant floor, and a single, terrifying question echoed in the deafening silence: Could our love survive the corrosive touch of greed?

I still didn't believe she'd actually go through with it.

Chapter 7: Coming Home

The strain of the past few weeks hung heavy in the air, a silent storm brewing between us. We'd fallen into a tense routine, punctuated by forced conversations and hollow smiles. Valerie hadn't mentioned the "exclusive content" again, but the unspoken tension lingered, a constant reminder of the chasm that had opened between us.

Thursday night arrived, and as I pushed open the door to our home, the weight of the day seemed to melt away. The familiar scent of my favourite stew wafted through the air, a stark contrast to the usual takeout containers scattered across the counter. Our house, usually a chaotic jumble of clothes and half-finished projects, was spotless. Even the stray cat, usually Valerie's nemesis, regarded me with a wary curiosity from the driveway next door.

"Hey," Valerie chirped, a wide smile plastered on her face. A smile that, quite frankly, felt a little too bright. I wondered if it could actually be genuine. She was setting the table, the clinking of silverware echoing in the oddly quiet house. "You're home early!"

"Traffic was lighter than usual," I mumbled, tossing my bag onto the couch with a wary thud. It felt like I was walking into a movie set, or some sort of other meticulously crafted scene.

"Great! More time to enjoy this deliciousness!" Valerie gestured towards the steaming stew, a dish she usually relegated to "special occasions" – occasions that rarely happened anymore.

She pulled out a chair for me, the gesture so uncharacteristic that it almost knocked me off balance. I sank into the seat, feeling like a guest in my own home.

"So," Valerie said, her voice a touch too chipper, "how was your day at the grind?"

The sarcasm wasn't lost on me. My "dead-end job," as she'd so delicately phrased it, was going terribly these days. Not only was it unseasonably busy, the stresses and pressures at work were seeping into my relaxation time at home. My art, the passion she'd once encouraged, had fallen by the wayside, a casualty of the growing tension between us.

"The usual," I muttered, picking at my stew with a growing sense of unease. "Meetings, emails, the soul-crushing joy of corporate life."

Valerie's laugh, usually bright and infectious, sounded strained this time. "Well, cheer up! At least you have benefits and a predictable paycheck. Unlike some of us freelance artists, right?"

The forced lightness of her voice did little to dispel the suspicion gnawing at me. This wasn't Valerie. This overly cheerful, overly accommodating version of her sent a cold dread pooling in my stomach.

"Actually," she continued, her voice dropping to a conspiratorial whisper, "work was pretty good today..."

She trailed off, her eyes sparkling with a secret excitement that sent a jolt of fear through me. This "good day" at work felt anything but. It felt like a confirmation of my worst fears.

I forced a smile, the taste of the delicious stew turning more bitter on my tongue. "New things, huh? Care to elaborate?"

Valerie hesitated, a flicker of doubt crossing her features before she plastered the overly enthusiastic smile back on. "Oh, you know, just industry stuff. Some streaming, collaborating..."

But the sparkle in her eyes, the nervous twitch of her hand, told a different story. This "collaborating" wasn't about building a brand, it was about crossing a line I wasn't sure either of us could come back from.

The silence stretched between us, heavy with unspoken accusations and a fear that seemed to hang in the air like a fog. As I stared at the woman across from me, a stranger cloaked in the familiar face of the woman I loved, the question resonated in the silence: Was this elaborate charade a desperate attempt to appease me, or a calculated move to soften the blow of what was to come?

My spoon clattered against the bowl, the sudden noise shattering the tense silence. "Collaborating, huh? With who?" My voice was strained, each word a tight knot in my throat.

Valerie's smile faltered for a fleeting moment, a flicker of nervousness crossing her features before it snapped back into place a little too quickly. "Oh, you know," she said, her voice breezier than usual, "just some folks from the platform. Networking, building connections."

The forced casualness of her response did little to quell my suspicions. "Names?" I pressed, my gaze holding hers with a steely intensity.

She hesitated, a flicker of defiance entering her eyes before she sighed. "Kevin," she mumbled, the name falling from her lips like a confession.

Kevin. The name itself was a punch to the gut. Kevin, the stupid friend of Amy's that she'd wanted to work with. My stomach churned. I felt as though I could vomit. There was no way Valerie had just stumbled into some wholesome collaboration with that guy.

"Kevin?" I repeated, the disbelief evident in my voice. "Seriously, Valerie? That Kevin?"

"Yes, Kevin," she snapped, a touch of defensiveness creeping into her voice. "What's the big deal? We just made some content together. It was professional."

"Professional?" I scoffed, the bitterness dripping from my words. "Right. Because Kevin's brand of 'professional' involves very little clothing and a whole lot of..." I trailed off, unable to even voice the accusations swirling in my head.

Valerie's face flushed crimson. "It wasn't like that! It was tasteful, creative! We just... played on some tropes, you know, for the engagement."

Her explanation did little to ease the knot of worry tightening in my chest. "Tropes?" I echoed, my voice barely above a whisper. "What kind of tropes?"

She avoided my gaze, her fingers nervously picking at the tablecloth. "Just, you know, a damsel in distress kind of thing. But I, uh, I totally rescued myself in the end. Very empowering, actually."

Her words rang hollow. This wasn't about empowerment, it was about exploitation. Valerie, desperate to capture new subs and even more money for her channel, had crossed a line, a line that felt like a betrayal of everything we had.

"And how'd it go?" I finally managed, the question heavy with dread.

A hesitant smile bloomed on her face. "Amazing, actually. The views are already exploding, and the comments... well, they're really positive."

My stomach lurched. Views and comments. That's all that mattered now, apparently. "Amazing, huh?" I muttered, the word tasting like ash in my mouth. The image of Kevin, a man I didn't really know, sprawled across our bed with Valerie, in sickeningly intimate poses, burned behind my closed eyelids.

"Yeah," Valerie said, her voice a touch too loud, a forced cheerfulness that grated on my nerves. "It was a huge success. We might even do another one."

Another one? The thought was unbearable. I forced myself to breathe, to take in the familiar scent of the stew, now completely ruined by the churning in my gut.

"And the content?" I finally asked, my voice barely above a whisper. "What kind of damsel did you play exactly?"

Valerie's smile faltered for a brief moment, a flicker of something akin to shame crossing her face before it was masked by defiance. "Nothing too crazy," she mumbled, avoiding my gaze. "Just a little helpless, you know? Needed a strong guy to save the day."

The implication hung heavy in the air. "Needed a strong guy," I repeated, the words laced with bitterness. "In our bed?"

The silence stretched, thick and suffocating. When Valerie finally spoke, her voice was barely audible. "It... it just happened. We got caught up in the moment, the energy..."

Her words were a slap in the face. Our bed, the place where we'd shared countless nights of intimacy and love, had been turned into a set for someone else's gratification. The betrayal was a physical weight pressing down on me, stealing the air from my lungs.

"Valerie," I started, my voice hoarse with a mixture of anger and hurt. "Did you... did you have sex with him?"

The question hung in the air, heavy with accusation. Valerie flinched, her eyes welling up with a mixture of defiance and shame. A single tear escaped, tracing a glistening path down her cheek.

"Yes," she whispered, the word barely audible.

The confirmation hit me like a physical blow. My vision blurred, the room seeming to shrink around me. This wasn't just a transgression, it was a violation of everything we had built together.

The image of our bed, now a symbol of deceit, sent a fresh wave of nausea washing over me. I pushed myself away from the table, the chair scraping harshly against the floor.

"I need some air," I choked out, the words a desperate plea for escape from the suffocating weight of her betrayal.

I stumbled blindly towards the balcony, the cool night air a slap against my hot face. As I leaned against the railing, a sob tore from my throat, raw and uncontrolled.

Chapter 8: New Rules

The sunrise bled across the horizon, painting the sky in hues of orange and pink. I hadn't slept, the image of Valerie and Kevin intertwined in our bed was a relentless tormentor behind my closed eyelids. The balcony door creaked open, and I flinched, expecting another wave of betrayal.

Instead, Valerie stepped out, her face pale and drawn. She perched cautiously on the railing next to me, a silent offering of companionship, or perhaps an unspoken apology. The silence stretched, heavy with unspoken words and the weight of my anger.

"Look," she finally said, her voice shaky, "I know this is a lot to process."

I didn't respond, the lump in my throat making speech a herculean effort.

"But," she continued, her voice gaining a touch of defiance, "it wasn't all bad. The content... it was good. Really good. The views are insane, and the comments are positive! People are loving it."

Her words were like gasoline on the fire of my anger. "So that's all that matters?" I finally choked out, my voice raw. "Views and comments?"

"No, of course not!" she exclaimed, a touch too quickly. "It's the money too. We can finally..."

She stopped, the unspoken words hanging in the air – pay off our debts, quit our day jobs, live the carefree life she'd always dreamed of.

But at what cost? The dream had morphed into a nightmare, fueled by betrayal and a desperate chase for financial freedom.

"Look," she said, her voice softer now, almost pleading. "If this is really a dealbreaker, if you need... an outlet too, then..." She faltered, the words seemingly sticking in her throat.

My head snapped towards her, eyebrows raised in disbelief. "An outlet? You mean, you'd be okay with me sleeping with someone else?" The absurdity of the suggestion hung in the air.

"Well," she stammered, a new note creeping into her voice, a hesitant hope. "Sure, if that's what it takes!" She paused, before continuing, "Maybe this doesn't have to be a one-time thing. Maybe we can explore this together. We could create even more content, even better content. Think of the money, the freedom it could bring us."

The hypocrisy still stung, but a new layer of betrayal chilled me. She wasn't offering some twisted equality; she was proposing a twisted partnership, built on the ashes of our trust. This wasn't about love; it was about exploiting a newfound avenue for success, success that seemed to come at an exorbitant price.

"No," I said, my voice flat. "That's not happening, Valerie. I already told you it could ruin my career, permanently! This isn't some business venture. This is our relationship."

"But what do you want from me?" she cried, tears welling up in her eyes again. "I love you. And I appreciate that you've supported me til now. We could stop now, but what does that do?... This content, it can change our lives."

Love. The word felt hollow in the face of her actions. Love wouldn't have justified her betrayal, wouldn't erase the violation of trust. Love wouldn't erase the image of Kevin, but it also wouldn't erase the woman I loved standing before me, her eyes pleading for a twisted form of forgiveness.

"I don't know, Valerie," I said honestly, the weight of the situation pressing down on me. "I need time. Time to think, to process everything."

She reached for my hand again, and this time, I didn't pull away. But the touch felt different, electric with a tension that wasn't there before. The silence returned, heavier this time, filled with the wreckage of our trust and the uncertain path that lay ahead. As the sun climbed higher in the sky, casting its harsh light on our broken relationship, one thing was clear: The old rules no longer applied. We could rebuild, but only if we found a way to navigate this new reality. A reality where love, money, and betrayal were now a tangled mess, and the new rules were yet to be written.

Chapter 9: Non-fiction

The fluorescent lights of the office buzzed overhead, casting a sterile white glow on the endless rows of cubicles. It had been another soul-crushing Friday at the office, filled with tedious meetings and overflowing inboxes. All I craved was the comfort of my own couch, a cold beer, and a chance to forget the week's bullcrap.

The past week with Valerie had been a blur of tense conversations, tearful apologies, and hesitant attempts at reconciliation. We'd decided, or rather, I'd hesitantly agreed, to try to make things work. Her solution, however, felt like a twisted compromise. She'd tearfully apologized for crossing a line, for the betrayal, but then, in the same breath, advocated for continuing her "content creation" with Kevin. Her reasoning was the same – the financial freedom it promised, the chance to finally escape the drudgery of our day jobs.

I couldn't deny the allure of that dream. The weight of bills and student loans hung heavy on us both. But the thought of her continuing down that path, the intimacy it entailed, gnawed at me like a persistent ache.

As a compromise, she'd even suggested I "explore my options" too. The thought of dating another woman, while initially a slap in the face, had morphed into a strange curiosity. A way to even the playing field, as she'd so delicately phrased it. The irony of it all wasn't lost on me.

Lost in these swirling thoughts, I practically ran out of the office building, eager to escape the fluorescent purgatory. The drive home was filled with a strange mix of apprehension and anticipation.

Apprehension for the future of our relationship, anticipation for the cold beer waiting for me at its end.

Unlocking the door to our house, I was greeted by the familiar scent of takeout, a recent development in Valerie's attempt to win me back. As I dropped my bag on the couch, a low moan, unmistakably female, drifted from the closed bedroom door. The blood drained from my face, the cold beer a forgotten fantasy.

My stomach lurched. What could it be? It's not what I think it is.... Is it?

The air hung thick with the sounds spilling from the other side of the closed door. A low, throaty moan, unmistakably Valerie's, escaped into the hallway, followed by a deep, masculine chuckle that sent a fresh wave of jealousy crashing over me. Another moan, this one higher-pitched and laced with playful defiance, answered the chuckle. My hand hovered over the doorknob, the urge to barge in a war cry against the sickening fascination that kept me rooted to the spot.

Another wave of sound washed over me – a sharp intake of breath followed by a series of soft, wet kisses. My stomach clenched, a cold sweat prickling my skin. I pictured Valerie, her hair cascading down her back, her eyes locked with someone else's, someone who wasn't me. The image was both arousing and repulsive.

I tried the doorknob. Softly, quietly, wanting to catch whatever this was in the act... It was locked.

A low growl, almost primal, rumbled from the other side of the door. It was a sound I'd never heard from Valerie before, a sound that sent a shiver down my spine that was equal parts fear and something I couldn't quite place. Minutes bled into what felt like hours, the symphony of moans and gasps punctuated by the occasional murmur I couldn't decipher.

My beer felt heavy in my hand, the cold glass a poor substitute for the ice my churning stomach craved. I took a long, slow drink, the bitter liquid doing little to quell the storm within. Instead, it sharpened my senses, making the sounds from the bedroom all the more vivid.

"Oh!" A sharp gasp from Valerie, followed by a low groan that sent a jolt through me. My grip tightened on the beer bottle, knuckles turning white.

"There you go, beautiful," a man's voice murmured, husky and deep.

"God, yes!" Valerie breathed, her voice laced with a hint of desperation that both repulsed and strangely excited me.

I squeezed my eyes shut, the image of their tangled bodies burning behind my eyelids. The sounds continued, a rhythmic dance of moans and gasps, punctuated by whispered words which fueled the fire of my conflicting emotions.

The anger was a white-hot ember in my gut, a constant throb that pulsed with every groan. Yet, beneath it, a strange current of arousal surged. The raw honesty of the moans, the unfiltered desire in their voices, sent a primal spark through me. It was a tangled mess of emotions, a cocktail of betrayal and desire that left me feeling utterly lost.

"Fuck yes! Please fuck meee!" I could hear Valerie beg, followed by loud, clapping-like noises. I was in complete disbelief. My feelings were hurt, once again, all the way to my soul. But for some reason, my cock was getting strangely hard.

I remained frozen, an audible-voyeur to their intimacy, the beer warming forgotten in my hand. As I sat there, suspended in this bizarre state of turmoil, the sounds from the bedroom slowly began to shift. The moans became softer, more languid, replaced by contented sighs and the murmur of hushed conversation. The silence that followed wasn't comforting, but heavy with the weight of what had transpired. It was a new reality, a reality I wasn't sure I could stomach.

I was mad at myself for even considering the fact I might have partly enjoyed it.

Chapter 10: Shattered Silence

The silence had morphed into a suffocating entity. Every beat of my pounding heart echoed against the hollow walls. Each muffled giggle, each suppressed moan from the other room was a fresh shard of glass lodged in my gut. I drowned my sorrows in beer, the bitter liquid a poor substitute for the churning emotions. Hours, or maybe minutes, bled into one another, time warping into a meaningless concept in the face of this agonizing wait.

Finally, the sound of movement stirred me from my daze. A shuffling sound, a low murmur, then the unmistakable click of the doorknob turning. I braced myself, expecting the worst. The door creaked open slowly, revealing a figure bathed in the dim hallway light. It was Kevin.

He was fully dressed, a wry smile playing on his lips. "Hey there," he greeted, a touch of surprise in his voice.

Valerie emerged behind him, her cheeks flushed but her expression composed. Unlike the raw panic I expected, she seemed mildly surprised, a flicker of something akin to amusement dancing in her eyes.

"Oh hi hun! You're home already?" she asked, a hint of a playful lilt in her voice.

The sight of them together, the ease in Kevin's demeanour, sent a jolt of hurt through me. My tightly coiled anger struggled to find its voice.

"Thought I might grab a beer," I offered, my voice strained but surprisingly calm. "Figured you might be a while."

The casualness of my words seemed to disarm them. The smirk faded from Kevin's face, replaced by a flicker of something resembling apology.

"We were just, uh," Valerie stammered, searching for an explanation. "Catching up a bit."

"Right," I said, taking a long swig from my beer. The bitter liquid did little to soothe the turmoil within me, but the gesture felt strangely appropriate.

The air hung heavy, thick with unspoken questions and unspoken accusations. Kevin shifted his weight uncomfortably, the nervous energy palpable.

"Well," he started, clearing his throat. "I guess I should head out. It was... good meeting you, man."

"Yeah, you too," I replied shallowly, offering a hollow nod.

As Kevin disappeared into the hallway, a new thought struck me, a cold, chilling realization. The anger that had been simmering within me started to morph into something else – a hollow ache.

"So," I said finally, turning to Valerie. The words hung in the air, lacking the usual bite of confrontation.

"So," she echoed, her eyes locking with mine. The playful amusement had vanished, replaced by a mixture of sadness and uncertainty. In that shared look, a silent conversation unfolded, a question lingering unspoken: Where do we go from here?

I realized I was subscribed to Val's content. I got a notification on my phone about her having a new stream up. I got an idea, and wanted to see how she'd react.

"I want to see today's content. Show me the stream."

Valerie's cheeks flushed a rosy pink, a shade deeper than the one from moments ago. "Oh," she mumbled, glancing away.

The confirmation was subtle, yet undeniable. My gut clenched, a cold knot forming in my stomach.

"Can I see the video from today's session? You said you wouldn't hide anything from me." I asked, my voice calmer than I felt inside.

She hesitated for a moment, then sighed. "Alright, come here."

We moved into the bedroom, where I noticed a wet spot in the bed and the sheets strewn all over the floor. Valerie blushed. She pulled up the video on her laptop, her face averted as the familiar set filled the screen. It was just as I'd feared – she was with Kevin, being intimate on camera, laughing, groaning, and having fun.

I watched, each frame a confirmation of the betrayal that hung heavy in the air. But amidst the anger, a strange sense of detachment washed over me. The raw emotions I'd felt earlier – the fury, the jealousy – had dulled, replaced by a hollow ache and a numbing realization.

It was exactly as I'd feared, too. He wasn't just a muscular, good-looking guy. He had a big, long cock too.

I watched quite a bit of the footage. There was a good angle of her taking it from behind. It would have been sexier to me, perhaps, if this was just some random pornstar getting railed, instead of my girlfriend.

She blushed more, not knowing exactly what to do. She offered to shut it off. I turned her down.

I realized, after focusing on his dick going in and out of her, that it didn't look like he was even wearing a condom!

"Wait, you made him wear a condom, right?" I asked, very concerned.

"Relaxxxx... I have an IUD, remember?" She responded.

"Valerie, what the fuck?" I asked, pissed off about this.

"Calm down! It's sexier for the audience... and besides, I had him get tested."

I was still pissed off, but that calmed me down a little bit. I fast-forwarded, wanting to see as much as I could. I quickly skimmed most of the video. All the way to the end of it.

The video ended, the silence even more deafening than before. Valerie finally met my gaze, her eyes filled with a mixture of shame and defiance.

"There you go," she said, her voice barely a whisper. There was no confidence whatsoever in her words.

I turned to her, not knowing what to do. I was mad that I found this footage incredibly hot. I knew I did; thankfully my jeans were concealing my stiffy.

"I want to be here, whenever you do this." I said. Valerie looked absolutely stunned. "For your safety, I want to be here. Actually, I don't want to just *be* here, I want to be the one filming it," I insisted.

Her jaw dropped. I expected her to say no. I wanted her to stop all of this, but I figured this was the best way to do it. I knew she wouldn't stop if I asked. So I thought I'd just make it super uncomfortable for her.

"...Okay, I'll talk to him," she responded, hesitantly. "I guess we can do that."

What the hell had I gotten myself into?

Chapter 11: The Surprise

Another week or so went by.

The weight of a new day settled on my shoulders with each step towards the house. The air hung heavy with the city's evening heat, a stark contrast to the cold dread that coiled in my stomach. The events of the previous night replayed in my mind – the forced civility, the hollow ache of betrayal, the unanswered question of where we went from here.

As I reached the door, my hand hovered over the knob. Hesitation, a familiar visitor, settled in. But pushing the door open was a necessity, a confrontation I couldn't postpone any longer.

The sound that greeted me wasn't the usual silence. It was a low, guttural moan, unmistakably female, laced with a hint of desperation. My blood turned to ice. The sounds were coming from the bedroom, the door ajar just enough to reveal a sliver of light and cast grotesque shadows on the hallway wall.

My initial urge to barge in, to unleash the fury simmering beneath the surface, was replaced by a sickening curiosity. I found myself rooted to the spot, a voyeur to their intimacy. The sounds continued, a rhythmic dance of moans and gasps, punctuated by hurried whispers that ignited a fresh wave of anger.

I knew I had a right to be angry. We'd discussed that I should be around for this!

The anger was a physical sensation now, a white-hot ember pulsing in my gut. It clawed its way up my throat, threatening to erupt. But another emotion, a strange sense of detachment, held it back. I listened, a silent observer in a scene that felt both familiar and utterly foreign.

Minutes once again felt like hours. The sounds continued, a relentless assault on my senses. Shame burned in my gut, a bitter counterpoint to the cold detachment that had settled over me. How long had this been going on? Was this just another betrayal, a continuation of the previous transgression?

A sudden shift in the sounds jolted me from my paralysis. The moans picked up their pace. What really annoyed me were the giggles, and the sounds of what seemed like a pleasant conversation.

I knew then what I had to do. With a deep breath, I pushed the door open further, the sound echoing through the silent room. Both Valerie and Kevin smiled, their eyes wide as they stared at me. Valerie was riding Kevin, very slowly, whilst facing away from him. Her breasts were bouncing, almost staring at me like they were another set of eyes.

Valerie's face blushed only slightly, as I noticed the tattoo on Kevin's chest.

"Hi honey! Glad you made it, we've been waiting for you!" she smiled as she continued to fuck him.

My jaw dropped open as they didn't seem one bit remorseful. Had this truly been planned?

I stared down between her legs, they were wide open. I had a clear view of her pussy, and the perfectly trimmed, tiny landing strip above it. She continued slowly bouncing on his big member. She seemed eager for more. I couldn't stop looking at the sight before me. It was, as much as I hate to admit it, a great viewing angle.

"You weren't supposed to do this without me!" I said, upset about the whole situation. She just smirked back. "I know! That's why we waited for you. We're not filming, we're just warming up! I knew you were coming home, and that you wanted to play the director!" she teased. Both of them began to giggle. She turned back, meeting his face, as they kissed.

The sight of them so happy almost broke something in me. But the scene.... It was so hot. I could feel my cock getting uncontrollably hard.

"You planned this?" Was all I managed to choke out, the words laced with disbelief.

Valerie's smile faltered for a brief moment, but then it returned, wider, more mocking. "Maybe a little," she admitted, her voice dripping with a newfound confidence. "We figured it might spice things up a bit."

The flippancy of her words sent a fresh wave of nausea crashing over me. Spice things up? This wasn't some game, some experiment to reignite a dying ember. This was a blatant disregard for our relationship; a cruel twist of the knife.

Her breasts bouncing as she slowly rode him did something to me. They just looked so perfect. His hands traced her body, following along until he took hold of her hips.

"You ready?" He smiled, almost teasing her. "Yeah, I'm ready for everything," she grinned so wide. The two began to slowly, passionately, make out. He gripped her tighter as they kissed. Little by little, I noticed his pace accelerating.

Before we knew it he was fucking her brains out.

She made eye contact with me for most of it. "Yes! Yesss! Fuck me Kevin!" she called out to him. I hated hearing her utter another guy's name.

He did exactly what he was told. Seemingly well, too. He plowed her at a pretty quick pace. I wondered if I would have been able to maintain that same pace as long as he did. I was sure I could do it, but what threw me off a bit was how long it lasted. He could go that hard, for that long, without making a mess?

Valerie screamed out, her high pitched moans sounding almost like a bird's call. I could do nothing but take in the scene. They wanted to prove a point, and they were proving it.

I had thought that asking to be there would make it too uncomfortable for them to actually perform. Instead, they'd called my bluff. I thought at least one of them would have been thrown off by my presence. Yet here they were, using my own presence against me.

He drilled up into her, just how she liked it. "Yes! Yes! Fucking yes!" she said, followed up with "Oh God! I love it!"

I could do nothing besides watch her sexy body bounce on him. I watched his cock disappear inside her. A lot of the time, her and I made eye contact. It was as if she were dominating me from afar.

He kept plowing. And fucking. And stuffing her, just as they'd so clearly planned. It took a while, until we heard from him "I'm gonna cum!"

From that point on, he fucked her as fast as he could. She turned red in the face, gasping for breath. She could do nothing but moan. I feared what might be next. And it was exactly what I'd thought.

He just kept going. He didn't pull out. He ended up cumming inside her. Not just a tiny bit of it went inside her; all of it did. He filled her right up, and she smiled the whole time he did it.

When he finally couldn't move anymore, he left his cock inside, to fill her up with his remaining juices. They smiled at each other, and she smiled at me.

All he said was "Wow.... Good girl!" Before giving her one hard smack on her right ass cheek.

Chapter 12: Filming

"**A**re you ready to start filming, babe?" Valerie asked me.
I didn't even know what to say. I hadn't quite processed what had just happened yet. They expected me to keep going?

"Uhhh... yeah I guess," I hesitated, not knowing how else to respond. It was clear I wouldn't be able to get them to stop. And besides, some part of this had me secretly aroused.

She had me go over to her desk and pick up one of the high quality, DSLR cameras. I was nervous to even pick the thing up. I didn't want to break it, and I certainly didn't even know if I wanted to do this at all.

She went around the room, turning on the expensive light fixtures she'd bought to enhance her streams. To be honest, everything looked really good. Her nude body looked gorgeous in the light.

"Should we dress up in a bit of cosplay, or just go for it?" she smiled over at Kevin. He replied "Nah, I think they already got footage of that last time. Besides, we're already naked. Let's just go for it!" I noticed him smile at her, before shooting a sly little smirk my way.

"Sounds great!" Valerie replied eagerly. "Have you figured out how to use that camera, hun?"

"Not quite, can you show me?" I asked, as she came over to help. She grinned wide, before teasing me, "Oh, I can show you *everything*."

I blushed, hard. I could feel my face getting hot. I also noticed my cock tingling in my pants, pressing against the fabric as it was growing hard again.

She showed me through the menu, the ways to zoom in and out, and everything else I'd need to start shooting. "Don't worry, I'm sure you'll be the *best* cameraman," before winking and kissing my cheek. Again, my dick throbbed.

"Do you need some more time, or are you ready for round two?" she smiled as she spoke to Kevin.

"I'm good to go, let's do this!" he smirked as he came over and gave her a little pat on the ass. I was already hard and jealous.

"How do you want us, director?" Valerie teased me. "I... I don't know." I replied.

I think she knew that'd be my answer. She seemed to be living for making me uncomfortable. "Hmmmm.... How about me sitting on the bed, with him standing between my legs?" she offered.

"Sounds good to me!" Kevin chimed in, following her over to the bed as she spread her legs wide for him. "Ready to shoot, baby?" she smiled at me, loving every second of this.

"Yes," I nodded, my face again blushing extremely hot. "Count us in," she told me, which I did. Right away, he began playing with her tits.

The kissing began next. It was hot. So passionate, just like before. I could tell how bad they wanted each other. No wonder people paid for this type of content.

He wasted no time. He pressed his large head to her lower lips, gently sliding it back and forth. She was still wet enough for him to enter. Her jaw dropped, and she let out a near-silent gasp as he slipped inside her. He held her tight, so that she wouldn't be able to go anywhere. That's just what she'd craved.

A moan fell from her lips as he went deeper, taking what he wanted. He kissed her forehead, and for the first time made an audible comment. "Good girl," he said, beginning to pick up the pace.

She sighed, and the look on her face told me she was longing for him. This time, it was mostly them making eye contact. Oddly, it seemed a little bit romantic. They were either the best actors I'd ever met, or they were truly enjoying one another. I didn't watch much porn, but this might have been something I'd have jerked off too if I'd scrolled over it during one of my sessions.

They made long eye contact as he went deeper. She sighed from the pleasure. "Oh God!" she moaned while he held her tight, claiming her body as his. "Shhhh," he smiled, kissing her temple and then her ear. "Just take it."

And take it she did. She didn't do anything to impede him. All she did was act her slutty little self for the camera. She did her best to stay quiet, unsure if he seriously wanted her to be silent. She started moaning more. First trying to stifle it, but later, giving up.

That was perfect for Kevin. It only served to make him harder. He felt irresistible. He knew she had to have him. He loved being the one who was giving her pleasure, for all the World to see.

He wrapped his arms more tightly around her back, picking up the pace slightly, but not going quite as deep. He could tell from her reaction that she was enjoying the quickness of his thrusts. It proved Kevin was quite the pleaser - he did exactly what she wanted.

"Yes!" she cried out. Loving his every thrust.

"Yeah, you like that? You want more?" he smirked while teasing her playfully.

"Yes, please! Please give me more! Oh God, don't stop!" Her cries sounded just like they did when I'd plow her myself. My cock was so used to getting hard from those noises that I grew completely stiff. I wanted to pull it out and take over. I knew I couldn't.

Was it just a Pavlovian effect making me hard, or was I actually enjoying this? It felt like some sort of a sadistic punishment in a way. However, Val was super sexy, and it was like watching my favourite pornstar live in action. I'd never experienced anything like it until now.

His speed grew to be ferocious, and all she could do was moan, beg, and scream. Valerie looked so hot getting stuffed like this. I just wished I was the one doing it. I moved a little to the side, trying to get a better angle. I figured if this was gonna happen, I could at least give people their money's worth. Besides, that might at least benefit me in the end.

"Oh God, Kevin you're so big!" she screamed, wanting him to never stop.

"Mmmm, thanks baby!" He replied, gripping her so tight. I thought he was about to fill her again, but instead he suggested, "How about we give the camera a better angle?"

She smiled at me and said "Yes, let's!" I watched as he gently maneuvered her onto her side. After a moment, she seemed to get what he wanted from her. He laid down, also on his side, behind her. "Hold your leg up," he instructed.

I watched as he pulled himself closer, grabbing by her hips. She giggled, loving how he touched her. Then, his cock appeared in the gap between her legs. He lightly teased his large, stiff unit against her wet little slit.

"You ready?" he asked, eager to insert. "Always, yes," she smiled. She leaned back, trying to kiss him but the height difference and position made it a little awkward. After a quick kiss, he held her tight, and nailed her from behind in this side-by-side position.

Now she could smile at me and watch my facial expressions some more. "Yeah, you like that, don't you?" she teased me, having a little trouble adjusting to how rough and deep he was going in this position. I could only blush, and nodded slightly, not wanting to interfere with this or my camera work.

"Yeah, take it baby!" he ordered her.

"Ohhhh yesss!" she screamed, loving how he felt. This angle was pretty perfect. It gave me everything, a clear view of her landing strip, her long legs, her tight little box, and his nice long member, filling her. I knew the audience would love it because I was as hard as could be.

"Yeah, just like that!" he called out, pounding her and refusing to stop. She started to scream, "Fuck yes. Stuff me! Stuff me babyyyy!" The loud clapping sounds were audible, and I could hear how soaked her pussy was every time he inserted himself.

From that point on, she just screamed and took it. Very few moans were actual words. He looked like he was trying to be as rough as possible. I don't know if he just got so into the moment, or if he was trying to upstage me. Either way, he fucked her until the pale white skin all over her body was turning a pinkish-reddish hue.

"Ohhhh! Ohhhh! Ohhhh Gahhhhh!" she trailed off, unable to finish what was likely her calling out to God. I thought he would have finished by now, but I guess he was a guy who could just last a good while even while pounding. He was really giving it to her. What took them to the next step was when he choked her hard from behind.

Her face turned bright red. She could no longer speak. He still fucked her, mercilessly. All I could do was film, and watch her tits bounce while she took her aggressive partner.

The choking seemed to do it for him. He roared, "Ahhhhh! Fuck yeah!" and sped up to his maximum tempo. He didn't stop banging her. Nor did he stop the choking. I worried she might pass out.

"I'm cumming!!!!" he screamed, finally breaking the silence. "Ohh! Ahhh! Ohhhhhhh!! Oh shitttt!"

Again, he began to fill her up. He kept going, until it was all out of him. This time, he fell out of her a bit earlier than last. The cum was leaking everywhere between her legs.

I must have blushed so red, because he was smiling so wide at me. Valerie didn't react much. She gasped, and tried to catch her breath. It took her a long while. Eventually, she began to recover and seemed to process everything that had happened.

When he asked "Did you like that, baby?" It still took her a few moments to respond. "Yeah... it was amazing..." she said, unable to do much other than breathe.

I stood there, awkwardly waiting. I didn't want to upset them and mess up the shot. I recorded them, laying there nuzzling, his cum leaking from her little pussy, for several more minutes.

They didn't just stain the sheets with the mess, they permanently stained our mattress. They waited several more minutes before giving me permission to turn the camera off.

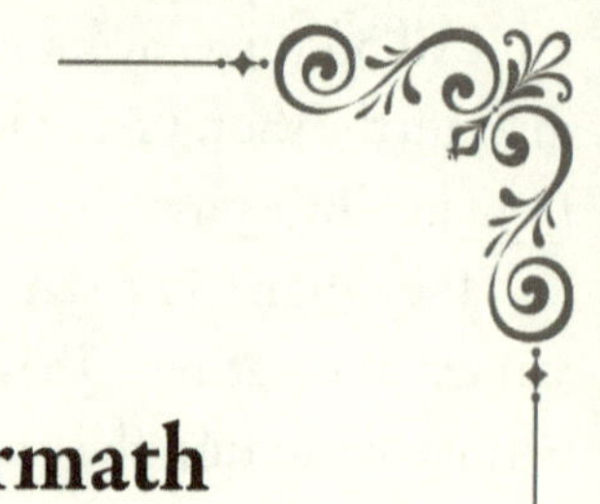

Chapter 13: Aftermath

The air hung heavy in the house, thick with the unspoken words and the lingering scent of sex. I stood by the window, the cityscape bathed in the cool light of dawn, a stark contrast to the turmoil within me.

A creak on the floorboards announced Kevin's departure. Relief washed over me, tinged with a bitter aftertaste. The slam of the front door echoed in the silence, a punctuation mark on the scene that played out just around an hour ago.

Turning around, I found Valerie watching me, a strange glint in her eyes. There was no shame, no apology, just a chilling nonchalance that sent shivers down my spine.

"Well," she drawled, pushing herself off the bed, "That was fun, wasn't it?"

"Fun?" I choked out, the word echoing hollowly in the room.

"Come on, don't be so dramatic," she scoffed. "We spiced things up a bit. Besides, those viewers deserve a good show, right?"

Her words scraped against my raw emotions. "Is this all a show to you, Val?" I asked, my voice tight with anger. "This is our life."

A sardonic smile played on her lips. "Our life is changing, honey," she said, walking towards me. "And it seems you're the only one who hasn't gotten the memo."

She stopped in front of me, her gaze holding mine. There was a new hunger in her eyes, a challenge I couldn't quite decipher.

"So," she continued, her voice dropping to a confident whisper, "Are you in or out?"

The question hung in the air, a crushing weight on my chest. Leaving felt like ripping out a piece of myself, but staying meant becoming a part of something I barely recognized.

The image of Kevin flashed in my mind, but this time, a new thought emerged. Could I turn this situation to my advantage? Could I use the camera, not just to document, but to expose, to reclaim some semblance of control? Was it really so bad if I could date others, too?

"...I'm in," I finally replied.

Valerie seemed to read the shift in my demeanour. Her smile widened, a touch predatory.

"Don't worry, sweetie," she purred, running a finger down my cheek. "You were a natural behind the camera. Consider yourself officially promoted to my personal cameraman."

My jaw clenched tight, but a spark of defiance flickered in my eyes. "Promoted?" The word held a new meaning.

"Yep," she chirped, her voice dripping with forced cheer. "Just be a good boy, alright? Follow directions, keep things interesting, and maybe, just maybe," she trailed off, leaning in close, "I won't make the punishment any worse," she smirked as she lightly tapped my cheek.

Her words were a threat. A sexy, albeit twisted, promise.

In that moment, I realized I was trapped in a twisted game, but the rules had changed. The future stretched before me, uncertain and fraught, but a seed of rebellion had taken root.

"Alright," I whispered, the word laced with a newfound resolve.

Valerie's smile widened, a victor's smirk. She took my hand, her touch no longer repulsive, but a challenge I was ready to meet.

"Good boy," she whispered, pulling me toward the bedroom. "Now, let's plan our next shoot. The viewers are waiting."

As we entered the bedroom, the camera clicked on in my hand, a silent observer about to become an active participant. This wasn't the future I envisioned, but it was mine to navigate. And who knows? Maybe, just maybe, the most captivating performance was yet to come.

If you enjoyed this story, please consider leaving a review! It really helps small artists and creators like me better understand my customers. I sincerely appreciate your time reading this book, and humbly ask you for an honest review. Thank you <3
-Ms Naughtee

Don't miss out!

Visit the website below and you can sign up to receive emails whenever Ms Naughtee publishes a new book. There's no charge and no obligation.

https://books2read.com/r/B-A-VGACB-BWRHD

BOOKS2READ

Connecting independent readers to independent writers.

Did you love *Hotwife: Streamer Girlfriend*? Then you should read *Cheating: My Unfaithful Wife*[1] by Ms Naughtee!

His wife belongs to another man... but not for long.

Cameron had it all—a devoted wife, a stable marriage, a life built on love and trust. Or so he thought. One anonymous message shatters his perfect world, exposing a truth too painful to ignore: Catalina, his beautiful, sensual wife, has been giving herself to another man.

The betrayal burns deep. Catalina has been sneaking off to hotel rooms, surrendering to the touch of her powerful, dominant boss while Cameron waits at home, oblivious. The thought of her in another man's arms ignites something dark inside him—rage, obsession... and an overwhelming need to reclaim what's his.

---

1. https://books2read.com/u/4A0E0k

2. https://books2read.com/u/4A0E0k

But when he confronts her, the air crackles with more than just anger. Jealousy fuels desire, and their passion reignites in ways neither of them expected. The tension is electric—raw, desperate, and dangerously addictive. As Catalina confesses her sins, Cameron is faced with a choice: walk away, or fight fire with fire. Because if she's going to play with temptation... so will he.

Cheating: My Unfaithful Wife is a steamy, pulse-pounding journey of betrayal, jealousy, and red-hot possession. This isn't just a story of heartbreak—it's an erotic battle of dominance, control, and the intoxicating hunger to reclaim what's his. The question is... when the dust settles, will their passion be enough to bring them back together?

Also by Ms Naughtee

A History In Love
A History In Love

BLACKED
Blacked Friday: A Cuck/Hotwife Novel
Black Friday 2: Blacker and Darker

Hotwife
Cucked 2 Book Collection: Backyard Pool Party & A Blast From The Past
Hotwife: Sexy Beach Vacation
Hotwife: Streamer Girlfriend
Cuck: Backyard Pool Party
Hotwife: Taking It All
Hotwife: Firefighter Fantasy
Hotwife: Halloween Hijinks!
Hotwife: Hypnosis Fantasy
Hotwife: Boudoir Photo Shoot
Hotwife: A Very Merry XXXmas
Hotwife: The New Year's Eve Party

Hotwife: Shared At Home
Cucked: A Blast From The Past
Hotwife: The St. Patrick's Party
Cheating: My Unfaithful Wife
Cheating: My Wife And Best Friend
Cheating: The Age Gap Affair
Cheating: My Husband Doesn't Know
Cheating: Behind Closed Blinds
Hotwife: The Tattoo Artist
Hotwife: At The Cottage
Hotwife: Cool Hiking
Cheating: The Boudoir Photographer
Hotwife: Hypnosis Hedonism
Cheating: My Neighbor's Son
Hotwife: Shared at Sea
Hotwife: Sexy Beach Resort
Hotwife: The Nude Beach
Hotwife: The Shower Scene
Cheating: Dark Desires
Cheating: Cold Revenge

Lesbian
The Christmas Party: A Lesbian Romance Novel
Lesbian: My Forever Valentine
Girls Trip: A Lesbian Fantasy
Lesbian Pool Party

Love Letters
Love Letters: A Young Love Story
Love Letters 2: The Second Chapter

Love Letters 3: A New Beginning

MILF
MILF: Crossing The Age Gap
MILF: On The Naughty List
MILF: The Babysitter's Secret
MILF: My Busty Neighbour
MILF: No One Can Know
Cougar: Single & Ready to Mingle
The Cougar and Her Cub: An Age Gap Fantasy
MILF: Eyes on the Prize
MILF: Full-Body Inspection
The MILF & The Pool Boy
MILF: The Cougar & Her Prey
MILF: An Unexpected Hookup
MILF: Public Seduction
MILF: A Wild Ride

Pregnancy
Pregnant: Suspense and Secrets
Pregnant: The Best Christmas Present

Threesome
The Threesome: MMF
Gangbang: By The Christmas Tree
Gangbang: A First Time For Everything
Sexy St. Patrick's Day: 2 Book Collection
Gangbang: St. Patrick's Day

Gangbang After Dark: An Interracial Smut Novella
Silent Springs Secrets
Gangbang: Til Dawn Do Us Part
Gangbang: At The Art Studio
Gangbang: At The Nude Beach

Trans
Trans Romance: A Dark First Time (M To F)
Trans Romance: A Friendship Gone Right (Or Wrong)
Trans Romance: My Old Crush

Standalone
The Genie of Love